FLO

Story by
KYO MACLEAR

Pictures by
JAY FLECK

Farrar Straus Giroux
New York

This is Flo.

Flo is the littlest.

Today she is exploring the
immense and mysterious sea.

HOP!
HOP!
HOP!
FLOP!

Now that her journey is done,
it's time to prepare for the day.

A good tune always helps.

SING, SING,
SONGS OF THE
GREAT HUMPBACK WHALE

Almost ready.

The other pandas are already ready.

They have been waiting for a while.

They wait while Flo
eats her breakfast.

Flo's favorite food
is strawberries.

Her number-one
saying is "Get floppy!"

Her best day is
Lazy Sunday.

But today is **not** Sunday. It's *Saturday*.

Which means: "Please, Flo. Hurry up.
It's time to get to the next bit."

"The next bit?" asks Flo.

So they explain.

Monday
Tuesday
Wednesday
French Club
Break Dancing
Beekeeping
Calligraphy Practice
Stamp and Coin Collecting
Gymnastics
Astronomy
Underwater Hockey
Medieval and Renaissance Club

WE ARE HERE
Thursday
Disco Society
Rock Climbing
Pottery
Friday
Fencing
Debating Team
Birding
Saturday
Unicycle Club
Tap-Dance Competition
Dodgeball
Motorboating

Flo, of course, has extra activities of her own.

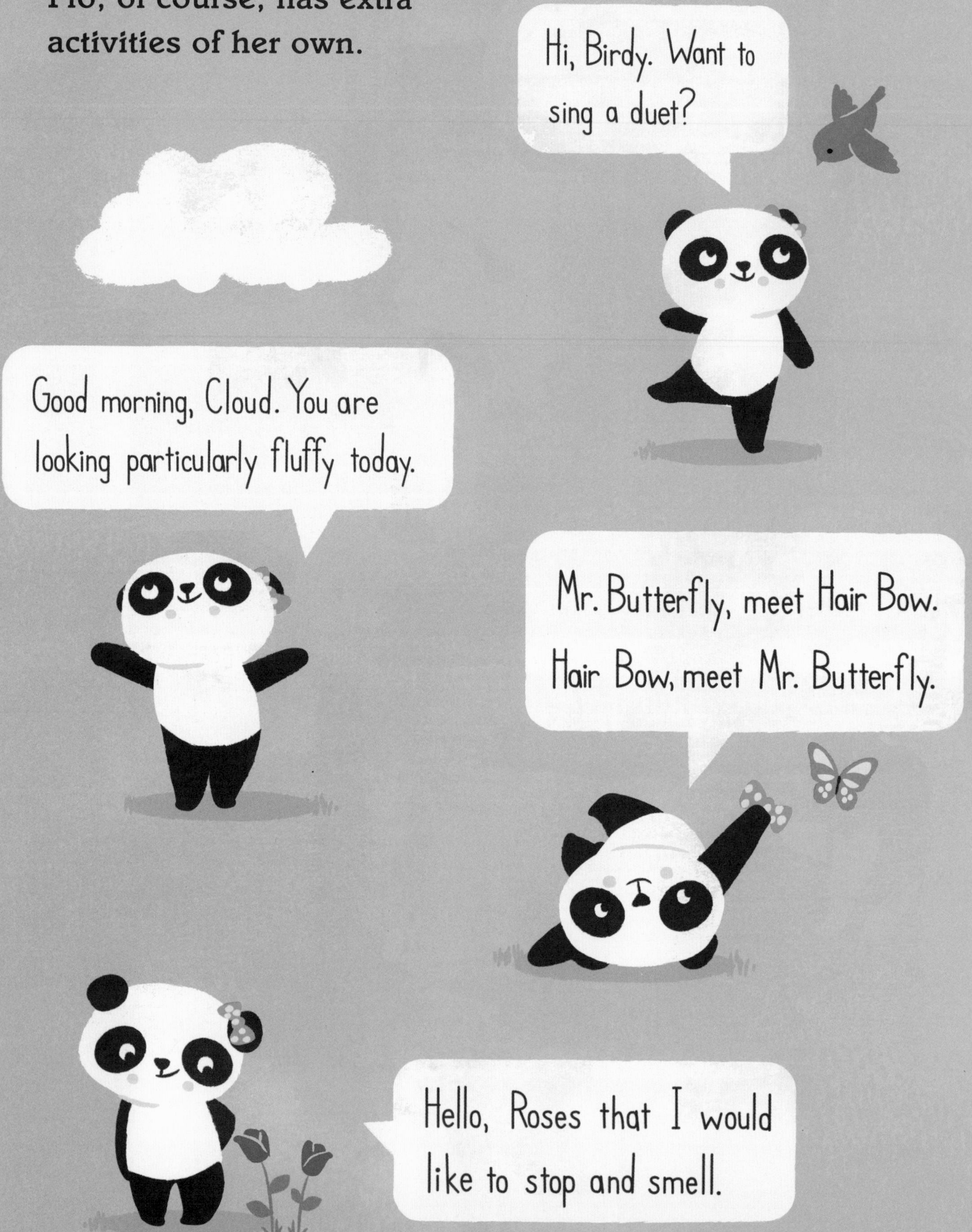
Hi, Birdy. Want to sing a duet?
Good morning, Cloud. You are looking particularly fluffy today.
Mr. Butterfly, meet Hair Bow. Hair Bow, meet Mr. Butterfly.
Hello, Roses that I would like to stop and smell.

8
Hello, Strange Ducky.

They try to be
patient, but
waiting for Flo
is not easy.

Luckily, Flo likes to play ball.

Throw the ball. Flo, throw the ball!
Please, Flo. Throw the ball.
Oh, never mind.

At the beach, the pandas decide to set off without Flo. They are fed up.

Flo plays a game with her friends.

Meanwhile, on the boat, the
engine has stopped working.

The pandas see that the shore
is not getting any closer.

They miss dry land. They
miss home. They miss . . .

QUACK, QUACK.
NICE WEATHER FOR DUCKS

"S.O.S.!" they shout.

But Flo isn't listening.
She is gone!

Flo has a rescue plan.
It's got height, bounce,
and many fancy ribbons.

It's got Flo.

Gracefully, the **huge** duckie
floats the pandas to shore.
The pandas feel the warm sun
and wind on their faces.
Flo feels the rush of adventure.

“Get floppy!” says Flo.
And that’s what they do.

Today is Sunday.
The pandas have
decided to do what
Flo likes to do.

They don't often
get to show their
floppy sides.

"Right, Flo?"

"Flo?"

"Hello, World.
I am Flo."

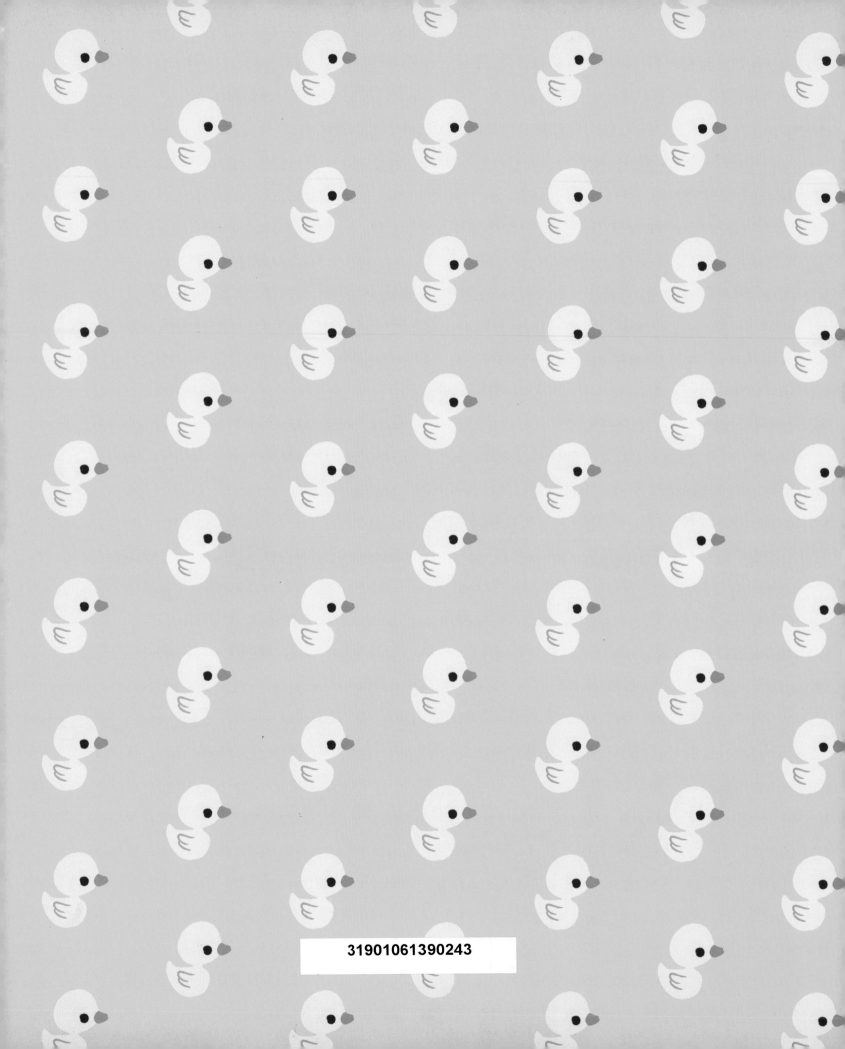